This book belongs to

_____

MINNIE'S SURPRISE TRIP

Disney's
READ and
GROW LIBRARY

Published by Advance Publishers
Winter Park, Florida

© 1997 Disney Enterprises, Inc.

Written by Wendy Wax   Edited by Bonnie Brook
Penciled by Phil Ortiz   Painted by Darren Hunt
Designed by Design Five
Cover art by Peter Emslie
Cover design by Irene Yap

ISBN: 1-885222-90-4
10 9 8 7 6 5 4 3 2

"Taxi!" called Mickey, waving his arm. A yellow cab stopped. Mickey and Minnie got into the back seat.

"To the airport, please," Minnie said to the driver. "We have a plane to catch."

The driver started the meter. "Where are you going?" he asked.

"Around the world," said Minnie. "The trip was a surprise Valentine's Day gift from Mickey. We'll have lots of time to be alone together."

At the airport, the driver stopped the meter. Mickey paid the driver a little extra for a tip.

"Have fun," said the driver.

Mickey gave the flight attendant their tickets while their suitcases were stowed underneath the plane.

The attendant smiled at Mickey and Minnie as they boarded. "Fasten your seat belts," she said.

Soon the plane began to roll down the runway faster and faster, until up . . . up . . . up they went.

Clump, clump. The wheels folded up into the plane.

Soon, they were so high that all they could see were big, fluffy clouds.

"I love to fly," said Minnie. "This plane is like a giant bird."

When they arrived in
New Orleans, they got their
suitcases. Then they went to
the streetcar stop.

Clang! Clang! A streetcar
pulled up beside them.

"Do you go to the paddle
steamer dock?" said Mickey.
When the driver nodded, Mickey
climbed aboard—but Minnie was
so busy taking a picture that the
streetcar left without her!

Minnie raced over to a tour bus. "Do you go to the paddle steamer dock?" she asked the driver anxiously.

"Yes," said the driver, "but that streetcar will get there first. Streetcars move on special rails so they never get stuck in traffic. This tour bus makes a lot of stops so the tour guide can point out special places."

When Mickey got off the streetcar, he looked to see if Minnie had arrived. "Maybe she's already on the boat," he thought when he didn't see her.

Mickey climbed aboard. At the back of the boat, he saw a giant paddle wheel. Steam made the paddle turn and moved the boat forward.

"Wait!" Minnie called, as the paddle steamer left without her. But only Mickey heard her.

"Meet me at the train station in Canada!" he called.

Minnie found a ferryboat that was just about to leave. She climbed aboard.

Minnie arrived at the train station before Mickey. She tried to find him on the crowded platform. But when the train sped into the station, she decided to climb aboard.

"It'll be easier to find him on the train," she thought.

"What a long train!" Minnie said.

"Diesel trains are very strong," said the conductor. "They can pull twelve cars at a time across long distances."

Mickey missed the train, so he decided to fly to Newfoundland on a helicopter. Of course, he arrived before Minnie did on her train. It was very snowy. He found a place to rent a snowmobile.

"I'll take a short ride," he decided. "Then I'll be back to meet Minnie's train."

Mickey sped across the frozen land.

Minnie waited for Mickey at the train station. When he didn't show up, she rented a pair of cross-country skis. "The snow's too beautiful to waste," she thought. "And I can use the exercise."

Suddenly, she saw some snowmobile tracks. She followed them, hoping they'd lead her to Mickey.

Mickey was having such a good time riding the snowmobile that he didn't get back in time to meet Minnie's train.

He saw a strange-looking plane that was about to land. The plane gave Mickey an idea, so he rode toward it.

When Mickey reached the water, he put his foot on the brake. He saw the plane land on the water.

"This doesn't look like an airport," he said.

"That's a seaplane," said a fisherman. "Seaplanes don't need airports. They have floats instead of wheels so they can take off from, and land on, water."

MINNIE, MEET ME AT THE CRUIS

"Can you fly a banner from that plane?" Mickey asked the pilot.

"Sure," said the pilot. "And I know where you can get one made in a jiffy."

A little while later, Minnie looked up from her skiing to see a seaplane flying overhead. There was a banner flying behind it.

SHIP. IT WILL TAKE US TO ENGLAND

Minnie giggled when she saw Mickey's message. She skied straight to the cruise ship dock.

Toot! The cruise ship was about to leave.

"Minnie!" Mickey called from the upper deck.

"I'll be right there!" called Minnie. But the ship was so big, she couldn't find him. After a while, she decided to go swimming instead. She had three pools to choose from.

Meanwhile, Mickey looked all over for Minnie and had no luck. Finally he went to the exercise room and lifted weights.

That night, he listened to an orchestra and watched people dance. He wished Minnie were there with him.

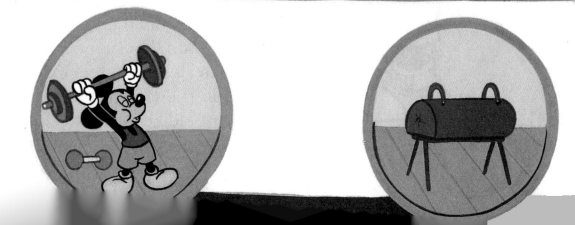

In London, Mickey and Minnie found each other at last.

"Let's go sightseeing," said Mickey. When Minnie agreed, Mickey climbed aboard a double-decker bus. He turned to show Minnie that the steering wheel was on the right side instead of the left side of the bus. But Minnie was outside, taking a picture of the bus as it pulled away.

Knowing that their next stop was Paris, Minnie went to the Hovercraft dock. "We'll just have to meet in Paris," she thought, giving her ticket to a crew member.

"I'm surprised this boat doesn't sink," she said.

"There is a cushion of air at the bottom of the boat that can hold a lot of weight," said the crew member.

Minnie arrived in Paris before Mickey did. She rode around the city in an underground train called the metro. It sped through tunnels, stopping at stations so people could get on and off. It was faster than buses and cheaper than taxis.

By the end of the day, Minnie knew the metro map by heart. She wished Mickey were there so she could show him around. But Mickey was nowhere in sight. He was on a boat, trying to get to Paris.

"This isn't Paris!" Mickey said
when he stepped off the boat.
"The roads are covered with water!"

"You're in Venice," said a man
in a long, black boat called a gondola.
"You must have taken the wrong boat."

"Oh, no!" Mickey said, frowning.

"Would you like a ride?" asked the gondolier.

"Sure," Mickey said. "It'll give me some time to think about what to do next."

As the gondolier moved the boat with a long pole, he sang to Mickey in Italian.

"Minnie would love this," said Mickey. "I wish she were here."

When Minnie didn't find Mickey in Paris, she decided it would be best to try to meet him at their next stop, China.

An hour later, Minnie boarded a jumbo jet. It had an upstairs, a downstairs, and even movie screens. Minnie wished Mickey were there.

Mickey had also headed to China. When he arrived, he decided to rent a green bicycle. The street was filled with people riding to work on bicycles. There were almost more bikes than cars!

When Minnie arrived in China, she rented a red bicycle. "Bicycles are good for the environment," said the bike shop owner. "They don't need gas."

"They are also great exercise," Minnie said. Then she got on the bicycle and rode onto the crowded street. She took pictures as she searched for Mickey.

DESTINATION:
SYDNEY, AUSTRALIA

Minnie didn't find Mickey, but she did find a cabin cruiser with a banner: DESTINATION: SYDNEY, AUSTRALIA. Since she and Mickey were supposed to go there next, she got a ride. She hoped she would find Mickey soon!

The family on the cabin cruiser was on vacation. They showed Minnie the kitchen and two bunk rooms.

When Mickey arrived in Sydney, he sent Donald and Daisy a postcard. He didn't mention that he wasn't with Minnie. He didn't want them to worry.

Then he went sailing. The sailboat had no motor. The wind made it move. Suddenly he saw Minnie on a cabin cruiser. Just then the wind died. Mickey was stuck.

"Thanks for the ride," Minnie called to the family. It felt good to walk on dry land again. When she didn't see Mickey, she went into a gift shop.

Minnie bought a postcard and sent it to
Morty and Ferdie. She didn't mention that she
was alone. She didn't want to worry them.

Finally it grew windy. Mickey sailed into the harbor. Minnie wasn't around, so he sat at a picnic table to think.

Suddenly, he noticed a pen on the table. It was Minnie's! Next to it was a note that had instructions for getting to Africa. Mickey knew that Minnie was headed to the next stop on their vacation.

When Mickey arrived in Africa, he bought binoculars. Then he rode in a hot-air balloon. Up, up, up he went.

"What makes the balloon rise?" he asked.

"The hot air," said a crew member. "There are burners that heat the air inside the balloon."

Down below were lots of giraffes and zebras.

Mickey looked through his binoculars and saw a jeep down below. Minnie was looking out the window, taking pictures.

"Minnie!" he called. But she was too far away to hear him.

He watched as the jeep bumped along through the jungle.

After taking lots of pictures of animals, Minnie looked up and took a picture of a hot-air balloon.

"Keep your head in the window," said the guide. "A pride of lions is up ahead."

Minnie wished Mickey were there to see the hot-air balloon. She didn't want him to miss anything.

Finally Mickey gave up. It seemed as if he'd never catch up with Minnie. Their trip was almost over.

He took a plane to Mexico to enjoy the sun before heading home. He hoped Minnie would be home when he got there.

Minnie had also flown to Mexico, the last stop before going home. She climbed into a kayak and began to paddle.

"I'll race you to that island," said a voice from behind her.

"Mickey!" Minnie cried. "Ready, set, GO!" she yelled.

Before Mickey could catch up, Minnie won the race.

"That's not fair!" Mickey said. He splashed her playfully.

Then Minnie took his picture. "It's great to see you, even though it's our last day of vacation," she said, giggling. "I have lots of pictures to show you!"

On their way home, Mickey and Minnie stopped to watch a rocket taking off from the space center.

"Ten, nine, eight, seven, six, five, four, three, two, one—BLAST OFF!" Mickey and Minnie counted. The rocket soared higher than any airplane could go.

Then Mickey and Minnie flew home on an airplane. Morty and Ferdie met them at the airport.

"Did you enjoy being alone together?" asked Morty.

"Well, being alone wasn't much fun," said Mickey. "But now that we're home, being together will be great!"

"Yes," added Minnie with a giggle. "My surprise trip turned out to be a bit more surprising than we had expected."